Tiya and the Minotaur
by
Constantine

Published in the United Kingdom by

Coalville C.A.N. Community Publishing
Marlborough Square,
Coalville,
Leicestershire,
England,
LE67 3TU

First Published in 2020

ISBN 978-1-9168960-8-6

Second Edition

10 9 8 7 6 5 4 3 2 1

https://coalvilleccp.uk

Mother said, 'Only the brave,
go on up to that deep dark cave,
high upon the mountainside,
for that is where the Minotaur hides.'

'Every year on Midsummer Day,
The big strong men go that way.
With weapons raised as one, they sing,
That they shall win a Minotaur skin.'

But never once did Tiya[1] see,
those men return with anything.
They would sadly sing into the night,
of how the Minotaur won the fight.

[1] (Pronounced Tea-ya.)

'Mum,' said Tiya, 'tell me this,
here on Thira, we live in bliss,
here women are priestesses and queens,
in fact, we own… everything.'

'So, tell me Mother if you may,
why it is on Midsummer Day,
that a woman cannot take an axe,
and see if she can bring a skin back.'

'We live in peace,' her Mum replied,
'but men like war and love to fight,
so, on that day they have their fun,
without really hurting anyone.'

'But wise women worry; you should too,
whatever are we going to do?
If one day a skin comes back,
there will be no beast for the men to attack.'

Tiya laboured hard that year.
But as Midsummers Day drew near,
her thoughts turned to being brave,
and just what *was* in the Minotaur cave

The day before the Midsummer Feast,
she asked the High Priestess for leave,
to climb upon the mountainside,
and hunt for mushrooms far and wide.

The High Priestess was old and wise,
and looked at Tiya with knowing eyes.
She smiled upon her pupil bright,
and said, 'Go and seek what you might.'

Tiya climbed high that day,
Searching out the secret ways,
Until she found her way around,
to where she felt her fate was bound.

The cave mouth opened tall and wide,
and utter darkness lay inside.
She briefly thought of turning back,
but of courage, Tiya had no lack.

She took a step into the dark...
'Was that a noise?' She thought 'Hark.
Is that a sob I hear echoing,
From somewhere, deep within?'

She followed the sound and far ahead,
a tiny point of light was shed.
Creeping forward the young girl saw,
a burning torch upon the wall.

And under this, a huddled shape,
sobbing with every breath it takes,
Upon its head, it had two horns.
Oh yes, this was the Minotaur.

Tiya made the slightest sound,
and the Minotaur leapt up off the ground.
'Who's there?' He said, 'What do you seek?'
But despite his size, his voice was meek.

Tiya stepped out and bowed as she said,
'Why do you cry? What's in your head?'
'Why is it that you are so sad?'
'I was told you were big and so bad.'

The Minotaur took a breath so deep,
as another tear rolled down his cheek,
he said 'I'm no monster, look at my head!
It's *grass* I love to eat, not flesh.'

'It's been my lot now for many years,
to guard this cave from all who come near,
and I know tomorrow, on Midsummer Day,
your warriors will be coming this way.'

Said Tiya, 'so tell me... Why do you stay?
Why not go somewhere far away?
Somewhere you will be safe after all,
and nobody's heard of a Minotaur?'

Minotaur said 'My girl so brave,
don't you know there's a secret in my cave?
Your men try to break in time after time,
but the secret, none of them could find.

What I guard is my people's future and past,
could it be you? Has the time come at last?
Don't you know little girl? Really? For sure?'
And with a flick of his hand…

He opened the door.

Behind the door lay a tunnel vast,
with walls and floor polished like glass,
reflecting a light from somewhere ahead,
a very bright light, all fiery red.

A blast of warm air shocked Tiya a lot;
wherever they were going was awfully hot,
but then our Tiya was awfully brave,
she took Minotaur's hand and led the way.

Before she got far, she started to sweat.
Minotaur thought, *"The poor girl needs a rest."*
He lifted her as gently as if she were newborn,
and sat her on his shoulder (She held on to his horn).

The tunnel ended and to Tiya's surprise,
she saw a circular chamber, massive in size,
Far above them the sky she could make,
And far below them, a fiery lake.

All this was enough to make anyone gasp,
more shocking to Tiya, looking round at last,
were all the Minotaurs, dozens or more,
all walking, playing, or doing some chore.

The Minotaur women's heads were adorned,
Minotaur children had corks on their horns,
there were Minotaur men all over the place,
Old ones, young ones. But of violence no trace.

All these people (mere monsters no more),
were nice to each other, no sign here of war.
Each one would smile at Tiya as she passed
and softly say, 'Has the time come at last?'

She couldn't call her friend "Minotaur," could you?
So she asked his name, he answered 'Kikeru^2,'
and he told her of the life that they lived,
deep in the mountain, where for years they had hid.

Mushrooms they farmed in caves far from light,
grass, wild veg, they would gather at night,
they sang, wrote, and had laws fair and just,
and for sport…

they liked to wrestle in the dust.

When Tiya saw this, a smile passed her face,
Could this idea bring peace to her race?
Instead of killing could they turn to sport?
'Must be worth a try,' the young girl thought.

She explained her plan and Kikeru said,
'Let's go see the elders after you've been fed,'
He made her a soup, a kind of mushroom stew,
Tiya took the recipe (Well you would have done too).

They saw the elders, tall fair and wise,
who sat in a chamber high up on one side,
Three males, three females, no one here was best.
They spoke with such grace that Tiya was impressed.

They looked at the girl, and smiles lit their faces.
they said, 'You're going to save both our races,
it was said if peace could be found one day,
a courageous child would show us the way.'

The following day, the Midsummer Feast,
the brave men went to fight with the beast.
But the cave was empty when they went in,
they scratched their heads, what a waste it had been.

But as they reached the bridge back to town,
dozens of minotaurs gathered around.
The men were scared, one lifted his axe,
when a voice cried out 'Wait, no one attacks.'

Forward stepped Tiya, out of the crowd,
her head held high and looking quite proud.
She said, 'Where are you going singing war songs,
and harassing folk who have done you no wrong?'

The men looked around, with fear on their faces
and saw that there was no chance to escape this.
Then another voice said 'Come men speak your case
While there is time, you have much need of haste.'

From under the trees, a figure approached,
as ancient as stone, but with heart strong as oak,
'High Priestess,' the men said, and bent at the knee,
This girl has betrayed us, our doom she's set free.'

The old priestess chuckled, 'Betrayed us men? Nay,
she came to me ere the break of the day.
If they wanted blood trust me, you'd be dead,
before you had the chance to rise from your bed'

'Come,' cried Tiya, 'the time is now,
for a peace that will last, and I know just how.'
She bought forth a cup of marvellous size,
made of gold & silver with gems down the sides.

'They will teach you a sport they call wrestling.
Each year on this day you may enter the ring,
and fight for the honour to bring home this prize,
which is yours for a year and your name is inscribed.

'So that in years to come whoever should win,
can look on the names of who came before him.
Can you think of a greater prize to bring back?
They will blunt their horns if you blunt your axe.'

The greatest man there walked out fierce and tall.
Straight up to Kikeru (the biggest after all).
He lifted his axe high above his head...
then threw it aside, 'It's a deal,' he said.

At the feast, Tiya was made a full priestess
(One-day high priestess, as I'm sure you had guessed).
The deal was ironed out and friendship renewed.
The Men's wine complimented the Minotaurs' stew.

In time both peoples became greater at that,
the Men learnt how to get water by tap.
Learned to build better houses, mine better ores,
and taught gardening skills to the Minotaurs.

For a thousand years, they lived in peace.
Though where they are now? Well, it sure beats me.
For a thousand years, they all lived in bliss.
On the island of Thira, sometimes called Atlantis.

The End.

Also, by the author.

Available now
in paperback, hardback and
on Kindle.

Coming 2023
in paperback and on
Kindle.

Tools to develop your child's creativity.

Find out more at www.thinkfc.org.uk

Freeing your imagination

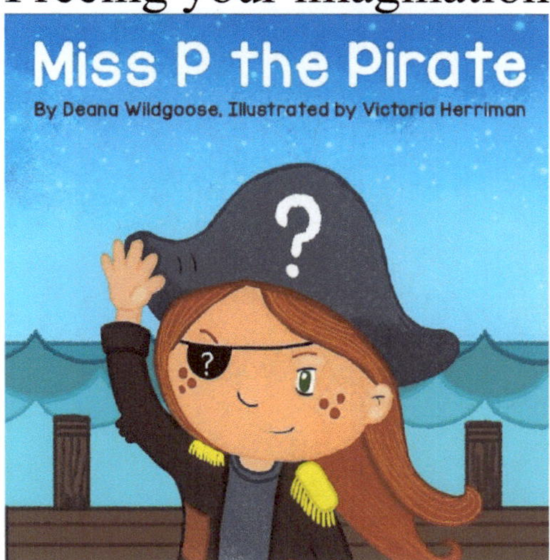

Sorting your ideas

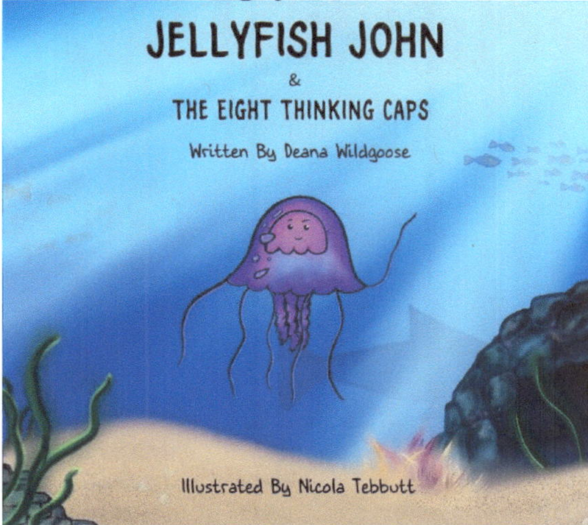

Exploring perspectives

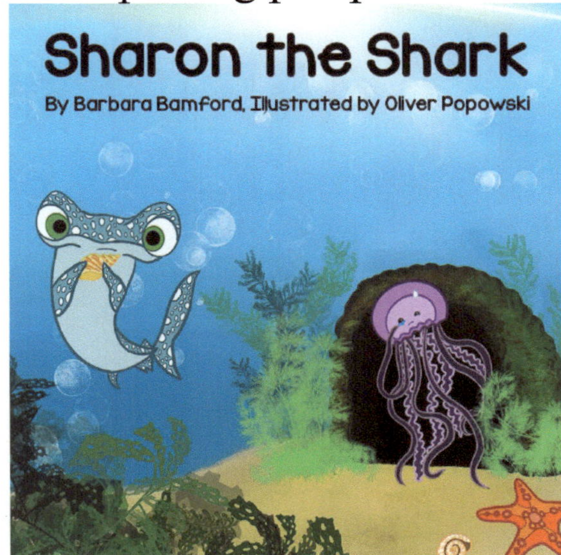

Developing helpful thoughts

What's next for Tiya and Kikeru?
Share your thoughts with Coalville C.A.N.
and you could see your idea in print.

Bring your Idea to Coalville C.A.N. Ground Floor, Memorial Square, Coalville LE67 3TU